One day in Africa, a new lion cub was born
to King Mufasa and Queen Sarabi.

A wise baboon named Rafiki
presented the new cub at Pride Rock.

The cub's parents named him Simba.

Lion King Word Search

Look up, down, across,
and diagonally to find these words.

MANZAI
~~MBESA~~
NALA
PUMBAA

RAFIKI
~~SCAR~~
~~SCAR~~
SHENZI

SIMBA
TIMON
ZAZU
ED

```
M P R S H E N Z I   I
N U S A M O N Z A   A
O M F R S U Z A Z   Z
M B R A F I K I N   N
I A N B S C M O A   A
T A T I C A R B   B
N E D L A W D N A
C L E P R A L A N
```

© Disney

Simba was a playful lion cub.

Simba, the playful cub, would reign over
his father's kingdom someday.

Simba met another cub. Her name was Nala.

Get Simba to Nala so they can play together!

START

FINISH

They played together every day.

Simba liked to catch Nala by surprise!

Nala was good at sneaking up on Simba, too!

The lions and lionesses of the pride
took care of each other.

But there was one lion who did not care
about the other lions.

Simba's uncle, Scar, wanted Mufasa's kingdom for himself.

Which picture is the real Scar?

(Hint: It's the one that's different!)

Answer: 3

Scar wanted to be rid of Mufasa and Simba.
He had hyenas do his spying and trickery for him.

"Stop!" Zazu cried.
The cubs were not permitted in the elephant graveyard!

But Simba didn't listen.
Scar had convinced him to go see the graveyard.

MATCH THE CHARACTER TO ITS NAME.

A
B
C
D

TIMON

SIMBA

NALA

PUMBAA

Answers: A-Pumbaa, B-Nala, C-Timon, D-Simba

Simba tried to roar like a fierce lion...

...but this did not frighten off Scar's hyenas!

But another roar frightened them!

"ROAARR!"
It was King Mufasa!

The hyenas fled into the mist.
King Mufasa told the cubs they had disobeyed.

That night, King Mufasa comforted Simba.

"Look at the stars!" said Mufasa. "The great kings
of the past look down from there and guide you."

"Remember that I will always be there to guide you."
"I will remember," said Simba.

WHICH ONE IS DIFFERENT?

A

B

C

D

Answer: B

Scar was furious that Mufasa had rescued Simba.

While Simba played in a gorge,
Scar ordered a stampede of wildebeests.

© Disney

Mufasa was nearby. He cried, "Simba! I'm coming!"

Simba clung to a tree during the stampede.

Mufasa tried to climb to safety,
but rocks crumbled beneath him.

"Help!" cried Simba.

WHO AM I?

LOOK AT THE CLUE BELOW AND GUESS WHO IT IS.
CIRCLE YOUR ANSWER.

SCAR   NALA
MUFASA   SIMBA

When it was safe to climb down,
Simba went looking for his father.

"If it weren't for you, your father
would still be alive," Scar said.

CAN YOU GET THROUGH TIMON'S MAZE?

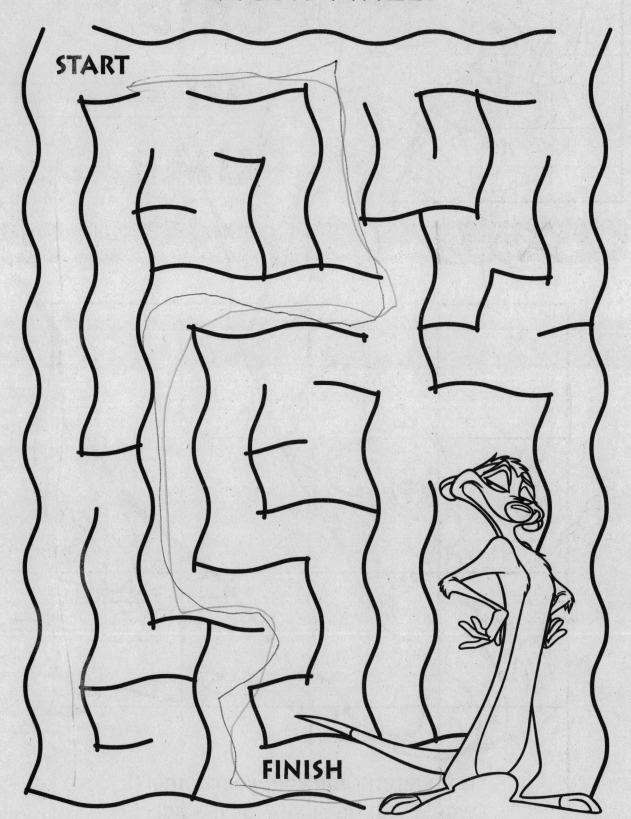

START

FINISH

USE THE GRID TO DRAW PUMBAA.

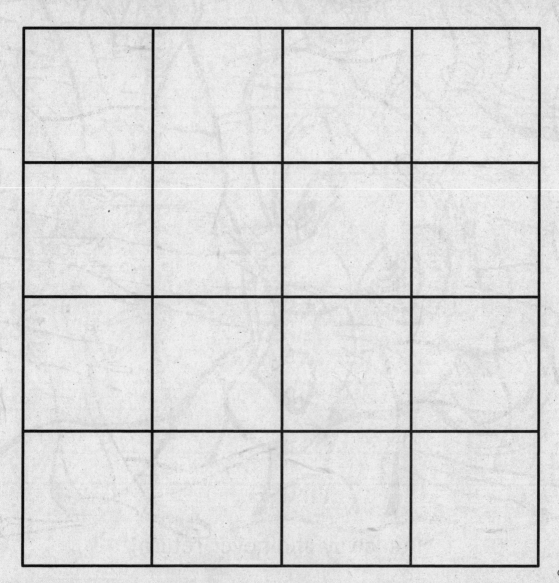

"Run away and never return!"

Simba did run away.

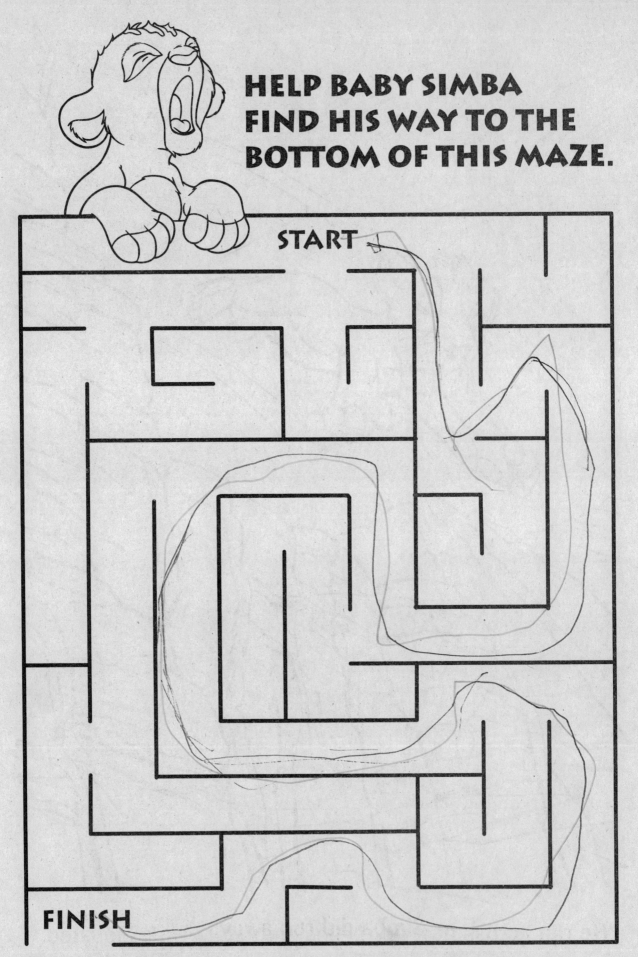

HELP BABY SIMBA FIND HIS WAY TO THE BOTTOM OF THIS MAZE.

START

FINISH

He ran across hot, dry plains and fell down exhausted.

Simba slept, and when he finally woke up,
a meerkat named Timon was staring at him.

"You nearly died," said Pumbaa, a warthog.

Help Timon and Pumbaa find the way to save Simba!

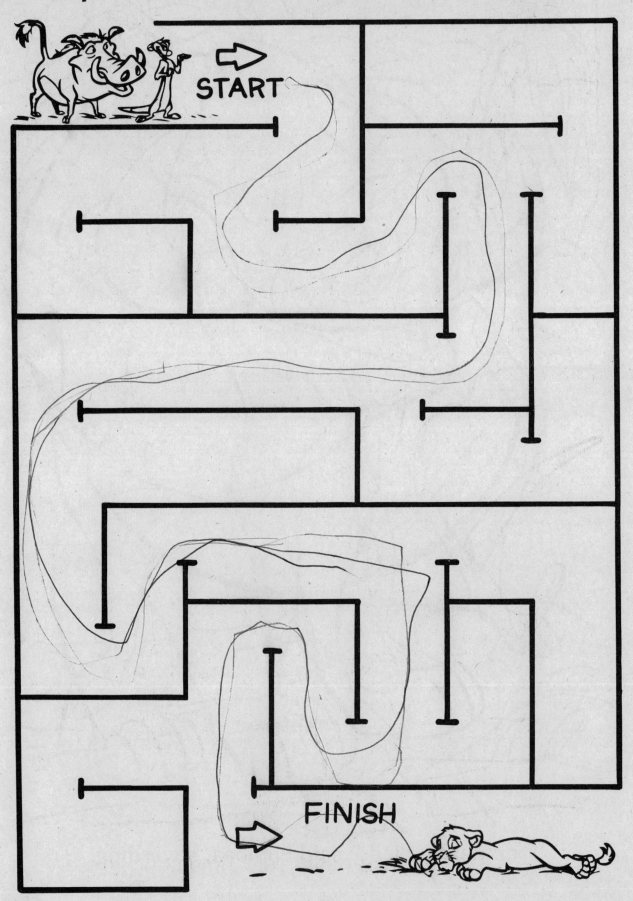

START

FINISH

"Stay with us!" said Timon.

Simba did stay with Timon and Simba...

...and he grew into a fine, full-grown lion.

"Hakuna matata—no worries!
That's how we live!"

"That's right! No worries!" said Simba.

"Pumbaa! A lion is approaching!" cried Timon.
"I'll rescue Pumbaa!" roared Simba.

The lion turned out to be a lioness—it was Nala!

Nala told Simba about Scar's reign of terror
and begged him to return.

That night, Rafiki led Simba to a stream
and showed him Mufasa's reflection.

© Disney

Mufasa said: "Simba—you are the one true king!"
"I will remember..." said Simba.

The next day, Rafiki announced
that Simba had at last returned home.

Simba found that the Pride Lands were in Scar's control.
Hyenas prowled and animals were hungry.

Suddenly, Simba saw Scar!

"This is my kingdom," Simba shouted as he attacked.

CAN YOU ESCAPE SCAR'S MAZE?

START

FINISH

© Disney

After the fierce battle, Simba took his place
as the rightful Lion King, with Nala at his side.

One day, Rafiki presented a new lion cub at Pride Rock.

It was King Simba and Queen Nala's daughter.